D

To every kid that ever needed a source of inspiration when they felt like their backs were against the wall, remember that a positive attitude and hope will take you further than you could ever imagine.

This one is for *you*.

Part One

"Effort will release its reward only after you refuse to quit." My father repeatedly told me this throughout my years of growing up. I was never quite sure what he meant. I am 11 years old, yet my father treats me like I'm 30. Where I come from in Richmond, Virginia, you have to be mentally tough to survive the roughness of this city. My 8-year-old sister, Jada, and I haven't had much growing up, regardless of our parents' tireless efforts to provide for us. My father works two jobs to keep the lights on, and my mother works a night job occasionally cleaning office buildings, so on the nights she does work, I'm in charge of watching Jada until my father gets home.

"Kam! Jada! You'd better get moving so you can make it to school on time!" I heard my mother yell from the kitchen. I could smell the scrambled eggs and bacon that she was preparing for us as my stomach grumbled. I tried to place the covers over my head until Jada ripped them from over me.

"Rise and shine, Kam!" My sister shouted with a big smile on her face. "It's the first day of school, and I can't wait to show Cynthia my new outfit."

"No one cares about your first day of school outfit… and besides, it's too early to be this loud. Can you hear yourself?" I asked Jada with a puzzled look on my face. She could tell that I was annoyed as she danced her way into the bathroom to get ready.

I got out of bed and freshened up. I'm not excited for my first day of 6th grade, and I heard my teacher, Mr. Jones, was a mean and old grumpy man that doesn't like kids. This is very confusing because he works with kids.

Luckily for me, my best friend, Shaun, will be in the class with me.

Shaun and I have been friends ever since we were babies. Our mothers are best friends, so it's almost like we are brothers even though we don't look alike.

I finally mustered up the strength to roll out of bed and get ready. I grabbed my backpack and my doodle book with all my drawings from my room before heading to the kitchen.

"Here's your lunch money, make sure you do not spend it on anything except for lunch!" My mom handed Jada and I $3.50 each.

"Kam, make sure you leave that little doodle book of yours at home. I don't want to have to come up to the school because your teacher had to take it away again."

I've always loved to draw. I draw anything. It's a way for me to escape the world and any problems I have going on at home and be in my own little creative space. Sometimes, I create characters and imagine myself as them. My father tells me that's called being "vicarious*". Except sometimes, I actually wish that I was them.

"Have a good first day of school, and make sure you watch over your sister, Kam," My mom said as she hugged both of us on our way out the door.

As Jada and I walked to school, I started to think and ask myself why I didn't have nice things like many of the kids that I went to school with. I mean, my parents work all day and although I have a new first day of school outfit, I have on the same shoes that I had last year. I looked at Jada as she carelessly skipped down the sidewalk and then came to a sudden pause.

"Good morning, Mister!" Jada waved and smiled at a homeless man sitting in the alley.

I grabbed Jada by her arm. "Mom told you not to talk to strangers!" I shouted with her arm still firmly in my grip and continued walking. I could see a dark figure emerge from the shadows of the alleyway.

"Oh, don't worry… I'm no stranger and besides, I don't bite." The homeless man responded with a smile in a raspy but gentle voice. I noticed a missing tooth, creating a gap between his front teeth.

I looked back for a brief second and turned to Jada, "and he's crazy."

We arrived at the school, and I hugged Jada and wished her a good day of school as she skipped over to a group of her friends in the hallway. I walked through the hallway towards my classroom, Room B13. I heard someone yell my name from a distance through the crowd. I looked over and saw Shaun.

"Kam, my man!" Shaun walked over to me, and we did our signature handshake - a high five, low five then followed by a snap and point. "I'm so glad we are in the same class together, it makes the first day a little easier, ya know?"

"Yeah, I know what you mean, man," I replied to Shaun as we walked into the classroom and took our seats in the back.

"Good morning class! My name is Mr. Jones, and I will be your teacher this year. I'm excited to get the school year started, but there's one thing I want you all to do. If you are sitting in the back of the classroom, I want you to switch seats with someone else in the class."

I got up and moved my seat closer to the front of the room. As I sat there, I could feel somebody behind me staring at me closely, it was almost uncomfortable.

"Well… if it isn't the biggest loser I've ever met in my life," I heard someone whisper in my ear from the desk behind me. I looked back and saw none other than the meanest kid in the school, Ralph Green. People called him Bulldog, because of the resemblance. I could feel a knot forming in the pit of my stomach. I thought to myself, "out of all the seats in the classroom, I had to pick this one."

"What are you doing here chump? I thought you would've gotten held back in the 5th grade," Ralph mimicked to me.

Ralph and I have a long history together; we've been assigned to the same classes ever since kindergarten. I looked back to give Ralph a look of disgust and was immediately hit with a spit wad right between my eyebrows. The whole class started to chuckle underneath their breath. Embarrassing.

"Ow!" I screamed out. I saw Mr. Jones turn around as he looked over the top of his glasses. "Is something wrong Mr. Johnson?"

"No, sir." I responded. This is going to be one long school year.

I was so relieved to finally hear the bell ring to end the school day. In no time the hallways were flooded with students as I waited for Jada at our designated location to walk home. I looked up and could see the top of her curly head cheerfully smiling through the sea of students. I grabbed her hand to make sure I didn't lose her as we walked through the hallway and outside of the school.

"How was your first day of school? Are all of your friends in your class?" Jada asked with the biggest smile on her face.

Before I could respond, my eyes were stuck on the most beautiful thing I had ever seen in my life in the storefront window of a bike shop. So shiny, so beautiful, so smooth… The iRide 3000. The coolest bike on the market that any eleven-year-old could imagine.

"Kam…. Kam. Kam!" Jada yelled and snapped me back into reality. "You should probably put your tongue back in your mouth. You know momma and daddy can't afford to buy you that bike. It's $150! That's $150 worth of dollars!" Jada was right. I'd never be able to afford that bike, or any bike at that.

As we turned the corner to continue walking home, I noticed the homeless man sitting on the corner again.

"Excuse me mister, do you have a spare dollar that you can share with me?" The homeless man asked me.

"I don't have a dollar, sorry," I responded and continued walking down the street. This time with a tighter grip on Jada's hand so she wouldn't try to talk the man's head off again. "I'll take anything mister," The homeless man responded back. To get him off of my back, I reached into my pocket and grabbed a dime.

"This is all that I have, man," I said as I showed him the dime in my hand.

"I'll take it!" He responded with a huge smile. "And in exchange for your time, I'll give you this rock." The homeless man pulled out a rock from a large bag he had sitting next to him.

"I don't want your rock, man. I can get a rock anywhere, just take the ten cents," I responded.

"Oh, no Mister. This isn't just any old rock," the old homeless man started explaining, "this is a rock of GRATITUDE." He presented the rock to me in both hands, grinning from ear to ear.

"Gratitude? What do you mean?" I asked the man. I honestly didn't even know what gratitude meant.
"You take this rock mister. This will help you achieve anything you ever dreamed about in life.

You do have dreams, don't you?" The homeless man asked me with a puzzled look upon his face.

"Well, I do…" but before I could finish responding, the homeless man cut me off.

"Well, then you take this rock. Every day, you hold this stone in your hand and imagine yourself doing all the things you want in life. This will help you practice patience and the things you have control over." I took the rock from the homeless man just so he would leave me alone.

As we walked away, I looked back, and the
homeless man winked at me, tipped his hat, and
smiled. I could see his missing tooth from 30 feet
away. I started to walk off, but instead I turned
around to ask the homeless man how come he

doesn't use the rock? He seems to need it more than I do, but when I turned around, he was gone.

"So, you tell me not to talk to strangers but you take gifts from strangers?" Jada asked me, and I could tell she was being sarcastic. I rolled my eyes at her as I grabbed her hand and continued walking.

As we approached our apartment, I noticed a yellow sheet of paper taped to our door. I walked up to the door and removed the sheet of paper. "EVICTION-NOTICE" written in bold-red letters across the top. I walked in the house and could smell my mom preparing dinner in the kitchen.

"Hey Babies! How was school?" My mom yelled out from the kitchen.
"Good!" Jada responded as she ran in the house and gave mom a hug.

I walked back into the kitchen to give my mom a hug and handed her the paper that was attached to the door. As I handed it to her, I could see the look on her face change. "Oh dear…" my mom whispered underneath her breath. I could tell it wasn't a good thing.

"Everything okay, Mom?" I asked. My mother wiped her hands on her rag and looked back up at me and smiled. "Everything is okay baby."

I went back to my room and grabbed my doodle book. For some strange reason, I kept thinking about that rock and what the homeless man told me it was for as I laid in the bed on my back staring at the ceiling.

Gratitude? I don't even know what that means. I rolled over in the bed and pulled my dictionary out of my backpack.

grat·i·tude

noun

the quality of being thankful; readiness to show appreciation for and to return kindness.

As I sat in my room, I caught myself dreaming of that bike that I saw earlier. I closed my eyes and imagined myself riding down the street to Shaun's house to show him my new ride. It felt good. It felt real.

That night, I heard my father come in the house late from work. I came out of my room to greet him as he arrived, but he was already in the bedroom with my mother with the door closed. I could hear something coming from the other side of the door that sounded a lot like crying. As I approached the door closer, I recognized my Mom's voice, crying. I put my ear to the door to get a closer listen to what she was saying.

"Glen, if we don't come up with $450 for the rent in the next week, we are going to lose our apartment," I overheard my mom whisper through her crying to my father.

"Don't worry baby, there's plans for us to work overtime next week that should be able to cover the rent," My dad replied. "I'll give the office a call in the morning and see if we can set up a payment arrangement."

I backed away from the door quickly. A wave of confusion and worry came over me. I thought to myself...

"Here I am wishing for a $150 bike, and my family is at risk of losing our home." The confusion and worry quickly transformed into a feeling of guilt.

I ran to my room and frantically searched for the rock that the homeless man had given me. I found it at the bottom of my bag and pulled it out. I held it in both hands in front of me with my eyes closed and whispered, "I am thankful for our apartment. I understand many people do not have a place to call home."

I opened my eyes and waited for a sign of my gratitude coming to life… nothing happened. "Stupid rock," I said to myself and placed the rock back on the top of my bookshelf. "I should have never listened to that crazy old man anyway."

I laid on the bed flat on my back staring up at the ceiling and continuously drawing in my doodle book. I looked over at the rock sitting on the bookshelf and noticed it had an unusual glow to it. I walked back over to it and held it in my hands, closed my eyes and was completely silent.

In my mind, I began imagining my family happy, together, and with no worries. I felt a slight smile come over my face as I put the rock back down and went to sleep for the night.

I woke up the next morning in a much better mood than the first day of school. I didn't understand why. My family was close to losing our apartment, and I still had to go to school and sit in front of Ralph Green all day. As Jada and I walked to school, I noticed the homeless man still sitting there. As we approached him, he turned around and waved to us with a huge smile on his face. I had to ask, "I don't get it, you are homeless and every time I walk past you, you seem to be so happy. What are you so happy about?"

The homeless man began laughing hysterically. This confused me, "What's so funny?" I asked.

The homeless man replied, "Well, Sir. I have everything that I need here. You see, it appears that I have nothing, but in all actuality, I have everything that I need as long as I'm happy."

This confused me even more. I could feel Jada tugging on my arm, "we are going to be late for school, Kam!" We began walking away from the homeless man. "Oh, Sir!" The homeless man screamed out to me. "Take this note, will ya?" He reached out and handed me a folded piece of paper. I took it from him and continued walking.

Once I arrived at school, I spotted Shaun standing in front of our classroom door. "Tough luck sitting in front of Ralph Green, man," Shaun said to me.

"Tell me about it, this is like the worst possible thing that could happen." I shook my head as I replied.

"Oh!' Shaun yelled out and reached into his pocket. "I found this posted in the boy's bathroom, you should check it out." He handed me the paper and in big bold letters at the top of the paper, it read "Art/Creative Competition $500 Award."

I almost lost my breath. "This is right up your alley dude; I've never seen anyone as artistically gifted as you." Shaun encouraged me.

I continued reading and looked down at the date, "August 23rd, Shaun? That means I only have three days to put something together."

"You can do it man; I have faith in you," Shaun replied as he patted me on my back.

As we walked into class, I pulled out the folded piece of paper the homeless man had handed me.

"Great works are performed not by strength, but by perseverance. This week, you will be tested in new ways that will require you to be patient and brave," The paper read.

Before I could put the sheet back in my pocket, it was quickly snatched out of my hand. Of course, I look up, and it's Ralph Green.

"What do we have here? A wittle love letter for wittle Kam from his wittle Mommy?" Ralph mocked me, and all of the kids around pointed and laughed.

Before I could respond, Ralph was on to his next victim. "WHAT ARE THOOOOSE?!" Ralph pointed at the feet of a kid walking in the classroom with a huge hole in the front of his shoe. Again, Ralph's fan club began laughing uncontrollably. "Wholly, Moly! Are those the new Hole Jordan's?" Ralph continued to joke about the kid.

The kid put his head down and walked to the back of the classroom to take his seat. I could tell he was hurt by Ralph's jokes. I began to feel myself becoming angry, but I said nothing to defend him.

As I sat in the classroom, I started to think about what the note meant that the homeless man had handed me. I don't even know what perseverance means. I broke out my dictionary:

> **Perseverance** - noun - The quality that allows someone to continue trying to do something even though it is difficult.

That definition hit home for me. Nothing is easy where I come from. I don't have the same worries as the average 11-year-old. My worries consist of worrying about gunshots at night or wondering if my family will still have a place to call home when I get out of school… but this word, perseverance, is giving me a new feeling of hope.

When I got home from school, I finished my homework and immediately ripped my doodle book from my backpack and began planning the masterpiece I was going to create to enter in the art competition.

Hours passed by, and still my paper was blank. I started to feel the frustration come over me once again. "Stupid art contest. I'll never win anyway." I started to doubt myself. I looked over and noticed the rock had that unusual glow to it again. I walked over to the shelf and held it in my hands while closing my eyes. Images of inspiration filled my mind. One stood out in particular. A beautiful drawing of the buildings and downtown skyline.

Perfect, I thought to myself and put the rock back on the shelf. Maybe this rock really is magical. Maybe the homeless man isn't as crazy as I thought?

I began drawing the image while it was fresh in my head. Three and a half hours later, I finished.

"This is the most beautiful thing that I've ever created with my own hands," I thought to myself. A perfectly crafted drawing of the big beautiful buildings, bridge, and James River flowing in between them.

The next morning, I could not wait to get to school to show Shaun my drawing. I hopped out of bed at the sound of my alarm clock, quickly brushed my teeth, freshened up, and went to greet my mom for breakfast.

"Good morning, Mom!" I yelled out and hugged her then quickly took my seat and started eating. My mom gave me a strange look, "You're rather cheerful today. What's going on?" She asked.

Before I could respond, Jada interrupted, "I think it's a girl. Kam has a crush!" Jada giggled.

Jada has no idea what she's talking about, but I didn't waste my breath correcting her. "I don't know... Just excited for school today," I responded to my mom.

"Okay." She chuckled in disbelief and handed Jada and I our lunch money.

On our way to school, I spotted none other than the homeless man sitting in his same spot. I began to grow curious, "What is your name?" I asked the homeless man.

He looked up with that same smile as if he was happy to see me, "you can call me Mr. Smith."

"Okay." I responded and walked off.

"Oh, Sir! Wait a minute. Did you read the note I gave you?"

"Yeah." I responded.

"Good. Well what did you think?" Mr. Smith stopped himself and changed what he was going to say. "Take this note, if you don't mind... and remember what comes from the heart can never be stolen."

I took the note and continued walking to school excited to show Shaun my drawing for the Art Competition tomorrow. As I approached the classroom, I noticed Shaun standing in front of the classroom door.

"Shaun. Remember that flyer you showed me about the Art Competition?" I asked him.

"Yeah. It was only yesterday, dude," Shaun laughed as he responded.
"Well check this out... "I reached into my bag and pulled out the beautiful drawing.
Shaun's eyes lit up as he looked at it. "Whoa! Dude, this is awesome! Like it looks like Van Gogh drew it." Shaun yelled out in excitement as he held the drawing up to get a better look at it.

As he held the drawing up higher, somebody came from behind him and quickly snatched it out of his hands. I looked up and Ralph Green had it in his hands looking at it in amazement.

I could feel my heart quickly drop to the pit of my stomach.

"Well... Well… Well… What do we have here? This is a very pretty picture, did you draw this, Loser?" Ralph looked at me and asked.

"Yes," I said as I took a deep breath knowing Ralph had something up his sleeve.

"WRONG! I drew this, and I'm entering this in the Art Competition tomorrow to win my $500 cash prize." Ralph responded to me smiling from ear to ear.

"Ralph, come on, give it back to him." Shaun attempted to grab the drawing from him, but Ralph pushed him back instead. The bell rang and it was time to head to class.

I couldn't even focus in class; all I could think about was what I was going to do about getting my drawing back for the competition. There's no way Ralph will give it back to me. I felt something sliding around in my pocket. I reached in and it was the letter Mr. Smith, the homeless man, had given me. I unwrapped the paper and it read, "Sometimes, overcoming a challenge is as simple as changing the way you think about it."

This message was right on time. If I do not get my drawing back from Ralph, I'd have to come up with a Plan B.

The bell rang and school was over for the day. I met up with Shaun right away.

"Tough luck with Ralph, man." Shaun said, pointing out the obvious.

"I know. What am I going to do?" I asked Shaun.

"Well the good news is, Ralph won't be able to use that drawing in the art competition because you signed your name on it."

I just sat there and didn't say a word.

"You did sign your name on it…. right? Kam?" Shaun seemed very concerned when he asked me.

"I didn't," I replied as I buried my face in my hands. I felt like I could just cry right there in the middle of the school in front of everyone and not even care. I worked so hard on that drawing, and I wasn't sure if I could create something like that ever again.

Shaun could tell I was disappointed, so he put his arm around me and patted me on my back. "It'll be okay man. Let's look at the bright side. You are a great artist, and that drawing wasn't all that good anyway," Shaun joked and we both laughed down the hallway.

That night when I got home, I didn't waste any time getting to work on another drawing. I would think back about holding the rock in my hand and find motivation seeing happy images in my head of my family, stress free. There was only one problem, I didn't know what to draw. I reached into my pocket and pulled out the note from Mr. Smith again. **"Sometimes, overcoming a challenge is as simple as changing the way you think about it."** I turned the paper over on its back and noticed words on the bottom. "Life is like a bicycle. To keep your balance, you must keep moving."

Wow. I thought to myself. The only way to win the art competition now is to listen to my heart and not my doubts. I looked over at the rock, and it was glowing again. I held it in my hands as I closed my eyes. This time, I didn't think about anything. I just let my mind rest and listened to my heart for a change.

I pulled out a large sheet of blank white paper and went to work. Four hours later, my work was complete, and it was even more awesome than I could imagine. I had created a picture of a homeless man that looked a lot like Mr. Smith standing on the corner smiling from ear to ear with his hat tipped in his hand. In the picture, his clothes are dirty, his pants are ripped, and he's missing a tooth, but he is still happy. Over the top of the picture, I wrote the word, "**G R A T I T U D E**".

I was so impressed with myself that I wouldn't be happy with anything less than winning. The craziest thing about it is, I haven't even thought about how bad I wanted the bike, I just want to see my family happy and without worry.

The next morning, I woke up, and it was the day of the competition. The butterflies in my stomach were so strong that I couldn't even eat breakfast. As I grabbed my backpack to head to school, I noticed the rock of gratitude sitting on my desk. I picked it up and put it in my back pocket because I figured it would give me luck.

As I approached the school, I could feel the butterflies going wild inside of me. A lot of questions and doubts started to run through my mind. What if I don't win? What if I'm unable to help my family? What if the drawing that Ralph enters, wins? My mind was going crazy! I reached in my back pocket and held the rock tightly in my grip. Those doubts started to transform into confidence. I just want to see my family happy and without worry.

Part Two

When I arrived at school, I spotted Shaun in the hallway.

"Well…?" Shaun asked me. I knew he wanted to see what I came up with last night and if I was ready for the competition after school today.

I just smiled at Shaun without saying a word and walked into the classroom. As I walked up to my seat, I tripped over something and stumbled into my desk. It was Ralph's foot.

"I can't wait to win my $500 today! Thanks for the help, chump," Ralph sarcastically said as he laughed in my face. All the kids in the classroom laughed, but I was unbothered by it. I couldn't let it ruin my focus. I kept my game face as I took my seat.

During lunch, I couldn't even eat my food because I was so focused on the competition. I started to feel sick to my stomach, so I ran to the bathroom. Once I opened the bathroom stall door, I let out all of last night's dinner into the toilet. I could hear a noise coming from the stall next to me that sounded like sobbing or crying. I put my ear to the stall to get a closer listen.

"I'm so tired of people making fun of me and making jokes about my shoes and clothes," I could hear the voice in the stall next to me say through the crying. I took a step back and looked down at the stall next to me. I noticed the shoes immediately and the size 7 tag hanging out from the tongue of his shoe. It was Russell, the kid who Ralph made fun of because of the big hole in his shoe.

I felt bad and really wished I could help him out. I walked out of the bathroom stall to wash my hands and head back to the cafeteria. I got back to the table and just kept staring at my food. From the corner of my eye, I could see someone open up my juice box and take a big sip. I looked up, and it was Ralph walking by as he held up five fingers and whispered, "5-0-0."

Before I knew it, the bell had rung to end the day. I reached into my backpack to grab the rock. I couldn't find it so I panicked and dumped everything out of my bag onto the floor.

"Dude, what are you doing on the floor?" I looked up and saw Shaun standing over me.

"I lost my rock!" I exclaimed, trying to fight back the tears from my eyes.

Shaun's face showed so much confusion, "Rock? What Rock?"

I knew Shaun wouldn't understand, "Nothing. I'll tell you about it later. We have a competition to get to." I said.

Once we arrived at the auditorium, there had to be at least 150 people there. I could feel my gut drop as we took our seats.

"Good afternoon, students!" The speaker took the podium to explain to us the rules of the competition.

"Art, comes in many different forms. It is the expression of the creative mind. It comes in paintings, sculptures, poetry, and many more! We appreciate each of you brave students entering your beautiful pieces here today. You will be judged on three different things to win the grand prize of $500! Creativity, detail, and uniqueness. I will ask each of you to come up one by one along with your entry and give the crowd an explanation of your art piece and what inspired you."

The butterflies in my stomach started getting stronger. "Shaun, you didn't tell me public speaking was involved!" I looked at Shaun, and he could tell I was beyond nervous."

"Dude, I didn't know. I just gave you the flyer. You'll be fine man!" Shaun smiled at me and gave me a thumbs up.

I pulled out the slip of paper Mr. Smith handed me - **"Sometimes, overcoming a challenge is as simple as changing the way you think about it."**

Each student went up one by one and explained their beautiful pieces. I started to get nervous, these guys were really good!

The speaker went back to the podium to invite up the next entry. I gripped the edge of my seat so tight hoping that it wasn't me, that the blood almost stopped circulating through my hands.

"Our next entry, Ralph Green. Come on up Ralph." The speaker motioned to the crowd.

I could feel myself growing angry as I spotted Ralph walking up the steps to the podium. As Ralph took his place, I noticed something different about him. Ralph lost all of the color in his face, and I could see his hands trembling 30 feet away. Ralph grabbed the microphone and a loud screeching sound of feedback filled the auditorium, and I could tell it caught him off guard.

"Uhm... Hi. Everyone." Ralph shook intensely as he grabbed the microphone. Ralph bent down to place the picture on the display board and almost dropped it because he was so nervous.
"Thi..This. This is muh... muh... my drawing." Ralph paused. It was a long, awkward pause.

The speaker interrupted from the crowd, "Thank you Ralph. Do you mind sharing more information about the drawing?"

I had a feeling of enjoyment watching Ralph struggle on stage just knowing what he did to me and the way he treats others, but I also felt very bad for him and wanted to help him out.

Ralph began to stumble over his words again, "This is a pic.. picture of a river and some buildings."

The speaker continued to ask questions, "Ralph, do you know where this river and those buildings are?"

Ralph's face started to change colors, "Yes. Those buildings are here in the United States."

"It's the James River and those buildings are in Downtown Richmond, Virginia!" I blurted out from my seat and instantly covered my mouth. Ralph gave me a death stare from his position on the stage.

Everybody turned around to look at me as I sunk in my seat.

The speaker continued, "thank you for your time and submission, Ralph." He then continued up to the stage as Ralph walked off. "Next submission we have is from Kameron Johnson. Come on up, Kameron."

I could feel my chest tighten as I walked up to the podium. I placed my drawing on the display board and looked out at the crowd. The stage lights were so bright that I couldn't even see anyone out there. I closed my eyes for a second and thought about the the quote I read from Mr. Smith and imagined the feel and texture of the rock in my hands.

"Hello, everyone." I spoke into the microphone. My hands trembled as I placed them in my pockets. "My name is Kameron Johnson." I pointed to the man in the drawing, "This is Mr. Smith. Mr. Smith seems like he has nothing in this picture, but yet he's still smiling. I drew this picture because it shows that you do not have to have material possessions to be happy.

Happiness is inside of you, people may be able to steal things away from you, but happiness is inside of you. The beautiful thing about happiness is, someone can only take it away from you if you allow them to."

Complete silence filled the auditorium. I couldn't
tell if people were so impressed that they were in

awe, or if my piece was so terrible that they had no applause to give.

I exited the stage to return to my seat next to Shaun.

"So… How did I do?" I asked Shaun as I slumped into my seat.

Shaun wiped his eye, "Great man. You did great."

"Are you crying?" I looked closer at Shaun's face as I could see little droplets of tears coming from his eyes.

"No man. Of course not!" Shaun replied back to me, and we both started laughing.

It was finally time for the results as the speaker took the stage once more.

"Before we reveal the results, I will let it be known that the judges had a very, very tough time deciding on a winner as you all were very impressive! It takes a ton of courage to get on this stage and present your work in front of the eyes of strangers. For this reason alone, you are all winners!" Everyone cheered and applauded.

I was so proud of myself for taking a leap outside of my comfort zone that I really didn't care if I won or not. It was more or less a moral victory for myself. However, I still needed to win the money to help out my family.

"The 3rd place award goes to.... Julie Thompson and "The Beautiful Bumblebee!"

"2nd place, Julian Hill and "The Air Up There."

I held my breath bracing myself for the announcement of the first place winner…

"1st place, and the grand prize winner of $500…" I closed my eyes tightly.

"Kameron Johnson and "The Attitude of Gratitude!"
I couldn't believe it! Shaun and I looked at each other and gave each other the biggest high five! As I walked to the stage, I wanted to cry thinking about how an event as small as this had changed me life. To think, a homeless man living on the corner could have this kind of impact on my life. I walked on the stage, and the speaker handed me an envelope enclosed with $500 cash.

"Congratulations, Kid! Don't spend it all in one place!" The speaker smiled at me and shook my hand.

I walked back to my seat to grab my belongings and headed back home. I decided to take my usual path home, hoping to run into Mr. Smith and share the good news with him. As I approached the corner, I noticed a shadowy figure waiting near the lamp post. I approached cautiously, hoping it was Mr. Smith.

The figure emerged from the shadows. "That $500 is mine, Punk!" Ralph yelled out. I stopped in my tracks and ran as fast as I possibly could down the street in the other direction to hide in an ally. Ralph couldn't keep up as he bent over and started sucking air. I stopped for a second to catch up breath.

I felt a hand grab the back of my collar.

"Give up the money." I looked behind me as I was in the hands of Ralph's posse of friends.

Ralph came walking up, still out of breath. "You thought you could get away, didn't you? That money belongs to me. Give it up." Ralph said as he reached for the envelope in my back pocket.

Before he could grab it, I heard a familiar raspy voice yell out, "let him go!"

It was the homeless man, Mr. Smith.

Ralph and his posse scattered like rats. I got up, glanced at Mr. Smith and sprinted all the way back home.

As I walked in the front door, my mother was standing there. "Why are you breathing so hard, honey?"

I quickly lied, "Oh, just decided to get some exercise in on my way home today. So I ran."

My mother gave me a strange look, "...Okay, whatever you say sweetie."

I walked into my room, locked the door and opened the envelope with the money in it. I took a big sniff and smiled. I was so proud of myself, and I felt like I had to thank Mr. Smith somehow for introducing me to the Rock of Gratitude.

I decided the first thing that I needed to do was help my parents pay the rent. I took $300 out of the envelope and put it in a separate one. I snuck out of the house and headed to the leasing office drop box and placed the envelope with the money inside. The feeling of giving felt better than anything that I have ever felt before.

I was smiles all around at the dinner table. My dad came home from work with a confused smile on his face. He walked towards my mother and began laughing which turned into crying.

"What's wrong, Honey?" My mother asked my dad.

"So… Listen. Once I arrived home, I stopped by the leasing office to pay the remainder of the rent balance. The leasing agent told me someone already stopped by and dropped off an envelope with the money inside of it! I'm still so confused, I guess it's safe to say that we have an Angel looking over us."

My mother and father hugged and began crying from being overwhelmed with gratitude and enjoyment. At this point, I was smiling so hard my face started to hurt.

I took this moment in and thought to myself that I had to keep this going.

The next morning after breakfast, I told my mom I was headed over to Shaun's house, but I really went to the mall. I hated to lie, but it was for a good deed. I was hurt by the way Ralph talked about Russell's shoes. I headed to the shoe store and found the nicest pair of size 7 shoes that I could find. I paid the $100 and went back home.

After buying the shoes, I realized I had already spent $400 of my money leaving me with only $100 left. That's not enough to buy the bike. I always thought having money would solve all of my problems, but that wasn't the case. The act of giving made me far happier than having money. I decided Monday after school, I'd give the left over $100 to Mr. Smith. I figured he'd need it a lot more than I did. Besides, if it wasn't for him, I would've never had the courage to enter the art competition.

Monday morning, I got to school earlier than usual to leave the shoes on Russell's desk. I broke out my pen and a piece of paper to leave a note attached to the shoe box.

Russell,

You don't know me, and I don't know you. These shoes are for you. Enjoy them, but before you put them on, make sure you return the favor by doing something kind for someone else and shedding a light of happiness for someone that deserves it.

Sincerely,

Your Friend.

I walked out of the classroom so it wasn't obvious that I was the one that put the shoe box on Russell's desk. I didn't want to tell anybody about what I did for Russell. I didn't feel the need to, it really wasn't anyone's business.

Five minutes before the bell rang to start the day I went back to take my seat. Russell came into the classroom a couple of minutes after me. He saw the box sitting on his desk as soon as he walked in. He slowly approached the box as he took his seat. After looking inside the box, Russell smiled, put his head on his desk and silently started crying tears of joy.

I'm not a cry baby, but a tear came to my eye as I watched him. I felt really good throughout the day. As the bell rang to end the day, I was so excited to run into Mr. Smith and give him the envelope with money. I searched for Jada so we could hurry up and leave. Once I found her, I grabbed her hand and pulled her through the crowd of students.

"Why are you in such a rush! I didn't get to say bye to Cynthia!" Jada yelled at me.

"It's okay, just come on!" I replied back to Jada.

I arrived at the location that we usually see Mr. Smith. He wasn't there, instead there was a note sitting under a rock with my name on it. I opened the note up and it read:

"Whether you think you can, or think you can't -- You're right. When you give, you are rewarded in one form or another. Great work!"

I looked to my right and saw two bicycles there with me and Jada's names on them.

"Kam! Look! They have our names on them!" Jada screamed with excitement.

I stood still in disbelief.

I now know the feeling that Russell and my parents felt. The feeling that your good deeds haven't gone unnoticed.

I looked up and saw a well dressed man at the end of the corner that looked a lot like Mr. Smith. The man proceeded to tip his hat and smile at me. I noticed the missing tooth a mile away. I just smiled back. The feeling of change and inspiration took over as I felt a tear drop form in the corner of my eye.

I'm going to be alright. We are going to be just fine. This must be the feeling of gratitude.

Glossary

Vicarious- *vi-car-i-ous* – Taking the place of another person or thing; acting or serving as a substitute.

Perseverance- pur-suh-veer-uhns – The quality that allows someone to continue trying to do something even though it is difficult.

Gratitude- grat-i-tude - The quality of being thankful; readiness to show appreciation

Author Biography

I was born on August 3, 1990 and raised in San Bernardino County, California. I am a graduate of Old Dominion University in Norfolk, VA with a degree in Business Marketing.

I've been inspired to write ever since I was in grade school. Reading inspirational stories as a kid helped me to grow courage and confidence. My family did not have much while I was growing up, but my parents always worked tirelessly to make sure my older brother, sister and I always had enough. I lost my father at the age of 14 to cancer. This forced me to grow up at a much faster rate than many of my closest peers.

The year after the death of my father, my mother decided we were moving to Richmond, Virginia and took me with her. Although apprehensive about the move at first, I met many of my closest friends today. The youth is our future and it's up to us to help inspire and bring out the best in them.

Illustrator Biography

I am a 27-year-old, Richmond, VA native and Old Dominion University Alumni. I developed a passion for illustration and design during my early childhood years.

After years of creating, I knew my illustrations could represent more than lines on a paper so I decided to create only with the purpose of making art that tells an important message.

When illustrating and designing, I dream about various ideas, characters and concepts that can apply to the everyday life. My goal is always to use my positively impact others. If I can dream up symbolic ideas, and design vibrant illustrations that have substantial meaning, I believe that can make the greatest impact on the youth of our world and more.

Made in the USA
Middletown, DE
13 March 2018